1 to 100
Busy Counting Book

By Amye Rosenberg

A GOLDEN BOOK • NEW YORK

Western Publishing Company, Inc., Racine, Wisconsin 53404

1 tiny mouse,

2 fuzzy rats

3 creatures watch

4 napping cats

5 naughty mousies, **6** sacks of grain
7 fellows caught when it starts to rain

8 angels try to sleep on a cloud
9 noisy singers, **10** trumpets loud

11 girls a-fluting, **12** drumming boys
13 bells a-ringing—that's a lot of noise!

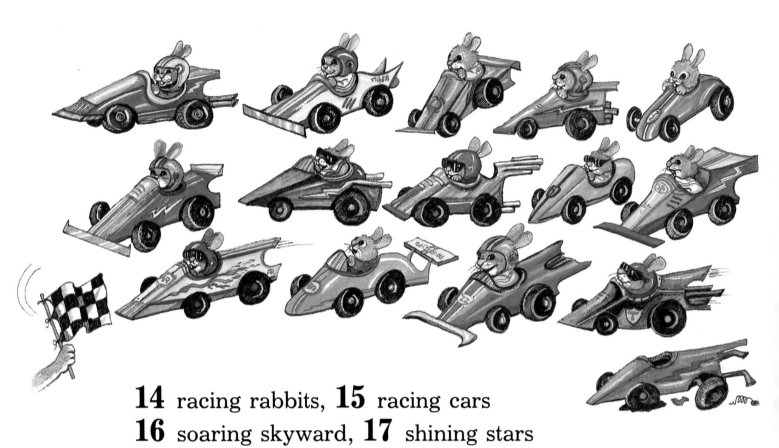

14 racing rabbits, **15** racing cars
16 soaring skyward, **17** shining stars

18 tumbling teddies
19 shiny hoops for
20 happy hamsters
But one *isn't* happy—oops!

21 pigs–away they go!

22 cats with faces aglow

23 woolly hats on their heads

24 chipmunks sliding on sleds

25 rabbits romp in the snow
26 snowballs—fun to throw!

27 beavers leap
28 hurdles steep

29 wagons carry a load
For **30** turtles on the road
With **31** suitcases full of things
And **32** sacks tied up with strings

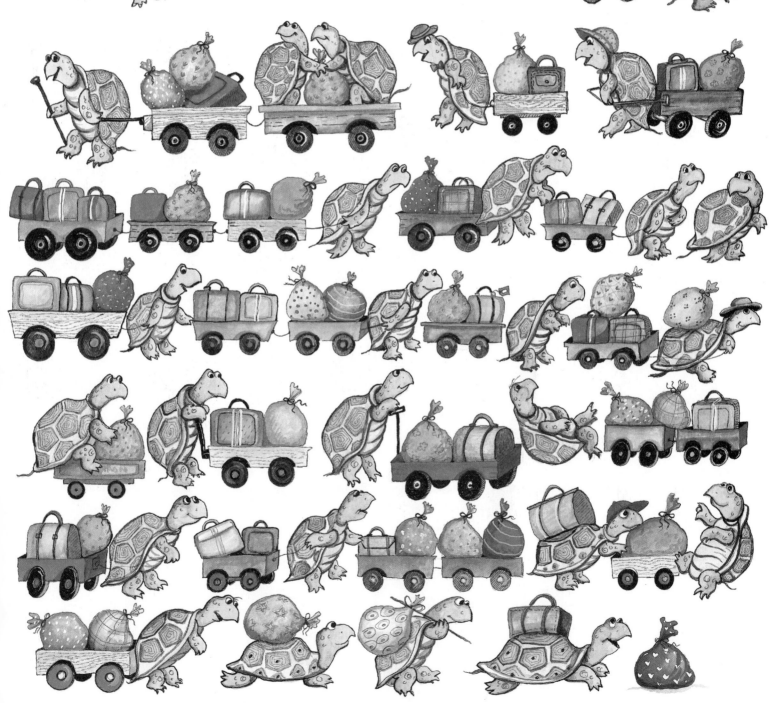

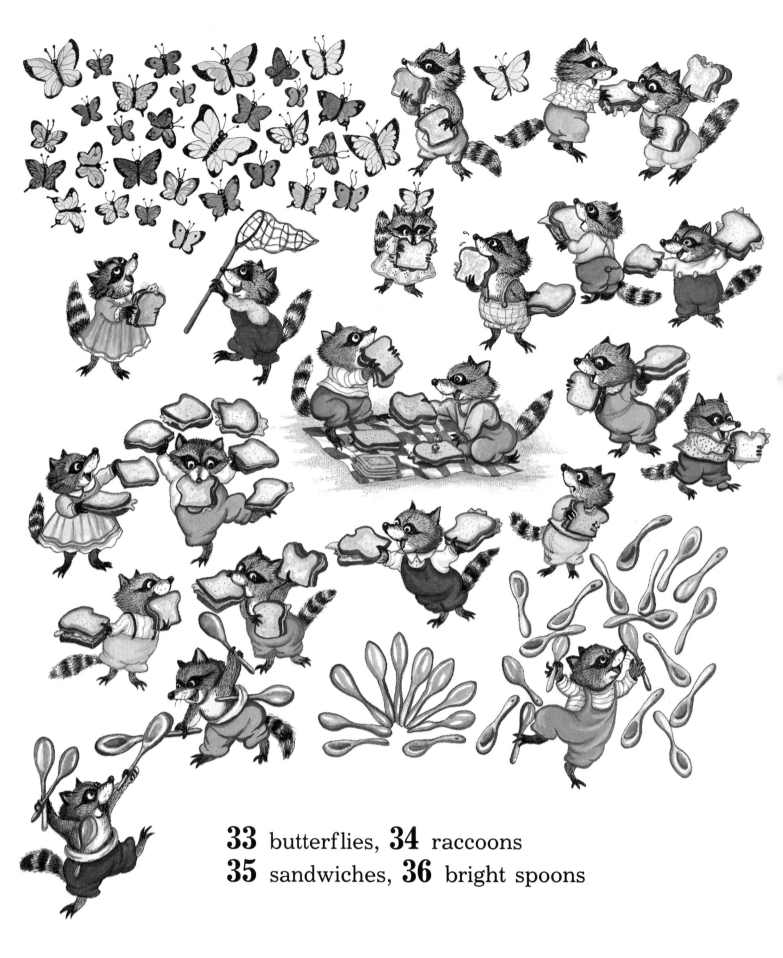

33 butterflies, **34** raccoons
35 sandwiches, **36** bright spoons

37 pudding blobs, **38** bowls
39 ants grabbing **40** doughnut holes

41 sunglasses, **42** toy boats
43 otters bob on **44** floats

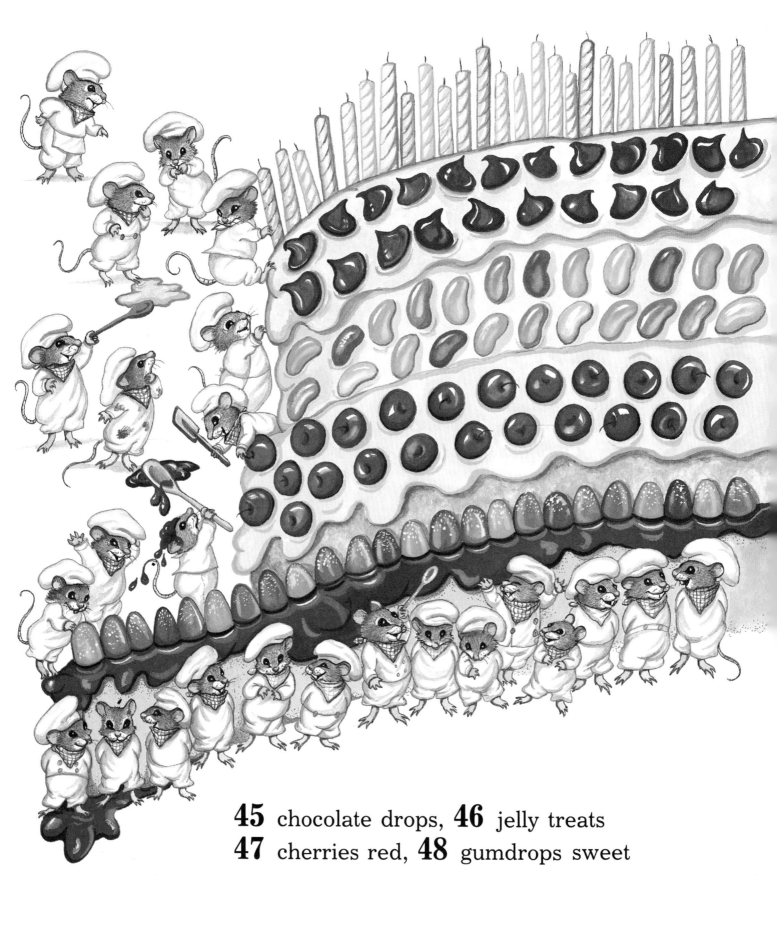

45 chocolate drops, **46** jelly treats
47 cherries red, **48** gumdrops sweet

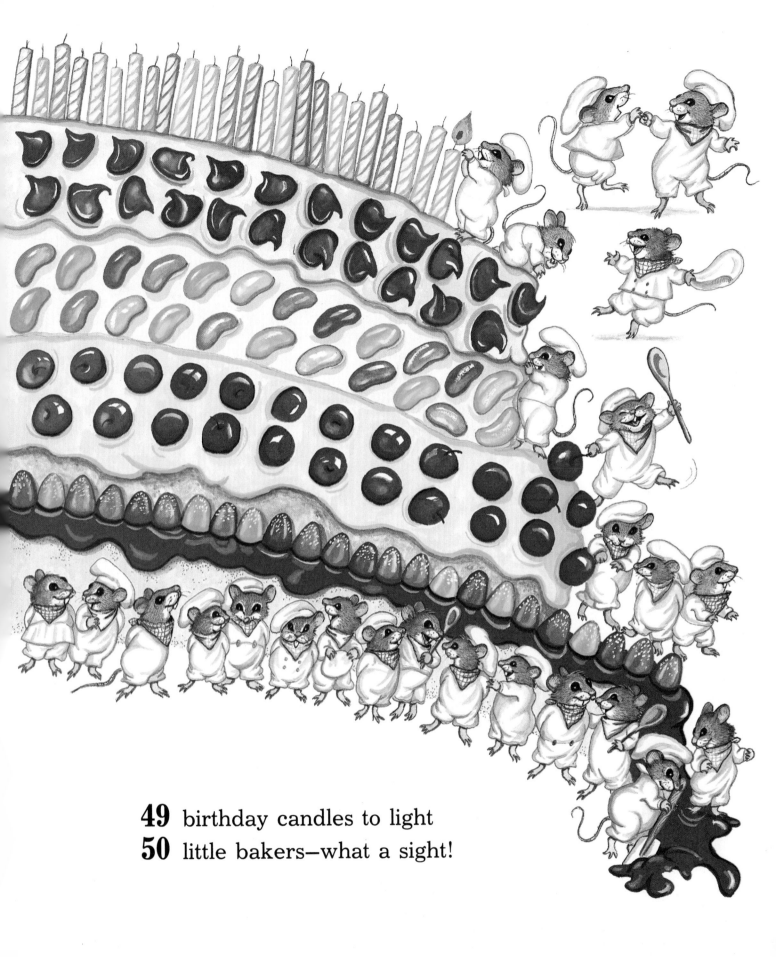

49 birthday candles to light
50 little bakers—what a sight!

51 out on Halloween night
52 jack-o'-lanterns burning bright
53 bats up in the air
54 bags of treats to share

55 fireflies, **56** spots
57 patches covered with dots

58 buttons on her coat
59 beads around her throat
60 pom-poms on her hat—
Count them in a minute flat!

61 raindrops fall from a cloud
62 umbrellas in the crowd

63 raincoats, **64** boots
65 hurry! The bus horn hoots!

66 sausages hung in a stall
67 oranges piled up tall
68 bananas, **69** peaches
70 lemons where nobody reaches

71 blue ribbons, **72** crows
73 packages they carry with their toes
74 letters with **75** stamps
Delivered in a hurry—that's why they're champs!

76 teeth, **77** peas
78 plums, **79** bees
80 flowers on their shirts
81 palm trees on their skirts
82 flags, **83** fish
84 nuts to munch when they wish

85 horns, **86** balloons
87 hats with **88** plumes
89 pants with stripes down the side
90 peewees marching in stride

91 striped shirts, **92** sashes
93 mice eyes covered with patches
94 hankies for seafaring sneezes
95 pirate mice waiting for breezes

96 frogs are smooth and green
97 watch the movie screen
Wearing **98** pairs of 3-D glasses
Eating buttery popcorn in **99** masses